Cherry Green
Story Queen

Annie Dalton

With illustrations by
Charlie Alder

Barrington Stoke

This book is for Vivian French,
a real life Story Queen.

First published in 2018 in Great Britain by
Barrington Stoke Ltd
18 Walker Street, Edinburgh, EH3 7LP

www.barringtonstoke.co.uk

This 4u2read edition based on
Cherry Green, Story Queen (Barrington Stoke, 2013)

Text © 2018 Annie Dalton
Illustrations © 2013 & 2018 Charlie Alder

A CIP catalogue record for this book is available
from the British Library upon request

ISBN: 978-1-78112-793-3

Printed in China by Leo

Contents

Chapter 1
Serious Magic

"Mia's doing it again," Billy said in a whisper.

Juno was painting her nails. "Mia's doing what?" she asked.

"*Wishing*," Billy said.

Juno looked at Mia. "How can you tell? She's just looking out of the window."

"Her eyes are closed," Billy said.

Juno went back to her nails. "She's just thinking."

"She's wishing," Billy said. "I can *feel* it."

Juno rolled her eyes. "And what does wishing *feel* like?"

Billy fiddled with the sparkly stud in his ear – the one he said was a diamond. "When it doesn't work, wishing feels *sad*."

"Mia's sad if she thinks wishes come true," Juno muttered.

Mia couldn't hear Billy and Juno. Her eyes were shut as she wished the same wish over and over. But when she opened her eyes, nothing had changed. She was still in Mrs Turvey's sitting room. She was still a foster kid.

Then she spotted Billy and Juno, and gasped. She'd been wishing so hard, she hadn't heard them come in.

"Were you wishing you could go to the ball, Cinders?" Juno mocked.

Billy shook his head. "She was wishing that she could live happily ever after."

Mia's eyes went wide with shock. "How did you know?"

"*Everyone* at Mrs Turvey's wants to live happily ever after," Billy said with a sad smile.

Mia didn't know what to say. She'd been living in the same house as Juno and Billy since the start of the summer. But she didn't *know* them. She didn't *want* to know them. At Mrs Turvey's, Mia felt like she was in the wrong story, a story with no happy ending. She wanted to find the *right* story, the one where her mum came back from the hospital and Mia got her real life back. All the other kids were in the story that Mia wanted to escape.

Juno held out her hand to admire her silver nails. "Looks like your Happy Ever After wish didn't work," she said. "Seeing as you're still here."

Mia's eyes filled with angry tears. Wishing had been the only thing she had left. It had been her secret. "It didn't work because magic isn't *real!*" she shouted, as she started to cry.

Juno gave her a funny little smile. "Maybe you aren't doing it right."

"What – what do you mean," Mia said.

Juno folded her arms. "Maybe everything isn't about *you!*" she said. "Maybe Billy would like to live Happily Ever After? Maybe you shouldn't hog all the magic for yourself."

Mia blinked away her tears. "I didn't *mean* to hog the magic."

"Yes you did!" Juno scowled. "You think me and Billy are, like, tragic *loser* kids that magic is too good for!"

Mia went bright red. Juno was *exactly* right. When Mia had made the Happy Ever After wish, she'd thought only of herself.

For a long moment, nobody spoke. One of Mrs Turvey's cats strolled in. Mia stroked the cat so she didn't have to look at Juno.

Then Mia had a wonderful idea. "Juno, what if we all wished *together*?" she asked.

"*Three* people wishing! That's *proper* magic!" Billy said, impressed.

Juno was never *ever* impressed. "But what if I want a different wish?"

"We just make the wish. The *magic* does the rest!" Mia said.

Juno grinned. "OK. But don't make me hold hands."

Mia giggled. "You don't have to hold hands! We'll close our eyes and I'll say the wish out loud. A wish for everyone at Mrs Turvey's."

Billy's eyes flew open. "Not Kyle?" he asked. "Kyle is *so* mean!"

"We've talked about that, Billy. *Everybody* wants to live happily ever. We can't leave people out," Juno said.

"We've got to wish for everybody, even Kyle," Mia said.

Mia felt all happy and hopeful. It had been so lonely wishing all by herself. But three kids, wishing together? That was *proper* magic, like Billy said!

Mia shut her eyes. "Please let *everyone* at Mrs Turvey's live happily ever after!" she wished. Then she looked at the others. "Now – wish so hard you see stars!"

Juno gasped. "I can see stars already."

"*And* me," Billy said.

Mia saw them too. Tiny gold stars danced behind her eyelids.

A warm breeze blew in the window.

It smelled like sunshine and roses and sweet spices.

"Mia, it's *working*," Billy whispered.

They opened their eyes. And the magic began.

Chapter 2

Who Is Cherry Green?

At first, it didn't seem like magic. They heard Mrs Turvey's gate swing open. Juno looked disappointed. "It's another foster kid."

A girl was walking up the path. She had long curly black hair and skin the colour of honey. Nobody was with her. No social worker. Nobody.

"If she's a foster kid, where's her stuff?" Mia asked.

All the girl had was a bright patchwork bag. As she passed the window, she gave them a cheeky wave.

'It's like she knows us already!' Mia thought.

"She's not a foster kid. She's magic," Billy said.

The doorbell rang and they heard Mrs Turvey laughing. "Ignore the dog!" she said. "Come in and meet everyone."

They looked at each other, amazed. A strange girl had turned up and Mrs Turvey was chatting and joking as if they were old friends!

"I *told* you she was magic," Billy whispered.

Mrs Turvey bustled in. "Juno and Mia, meet Cherry Green! She'll be sharing your room. Cherry, this is Billy."

Mia stared at the new girl as if she'd dropped out of the sky. She was sure she'd never seen Cherry Green before, but still she felt like she *knew* her.

Cherry had tried to seem normal. She had a normal name. She was dressed like a normal girl in a denim jacket, shorts and leggings. But, like a fairy-tale princess, Cherry had a magic shimmer.

'Who was this strange new girl? And where had she come from?' Mia thought.

"Girls, take Cherry upstairs and make her feel at home," Mrs Turvey said.

"I'll carry her bag," Billy said.

Mia and Juno led the way up to the front bedroom. Billy followed with Cherry's bag, and the dog and the cat followed Billy. Mia had never shared a room with anybody magic before. She felt a bit shy.

"That's your bed by the window," Juno said in a new, super-polite voice.

They were all shy, Mia realised. They had made a wish and a girl had appeared out of the blue. Nobody knew how to behave.

"You can use these two drawers for your stuff." Mia's own voice was super-polite now, like Juno's.

Cherry wasn't shy at all. "One will be fine!" she said, in a voice as natural and friendly as her smile. She unzipped her patchwork bag and took out clothes, a toothbrush, a brush and a comb.

"Is that all you've got?" Juno was so shocked she forgot to be super-polite.

"I'll only be here for three nights." Cherry gave them a little smile as if the four of them shared a secret.

'Will it take three nights to make us happy ever after?' Mia asked herself. She wondered if Cherry would say something about the wish. Maybe she wouldn't? Maybe she'd just get on with the magic?

But Cherry seemed happy to hang out with her new friends. "So how many kids live here?" she said.

"Six," Juno said.

Billy ticked them off on his fingers. "There's Mia, Juno, me, and Rosie and Riley. They're twins."

"You forgot Kyle," Juno said.

"I can't *ever* forget Kyle," Billy said.

"Don't you like him?" Cherry asked.

Billy shook his head. "He's mean and he steals things. You see my ear stud? It's a diamond that my real mum gave me. Kyle said he'd steal it while I was asleep."

"Kyle stole my photo of my mum and dad," Juno said.

"But I got it back for you, didn't I?" Billy said.

Juno nodded. "Mrs Turvey put it away safe. But Kyle says he can find it any time."

Mia expected Cherry to look shocked but she said, "Let's not worry about Kyle. Can you pass me my bag, Billy?"

"Isn't it empty?" he asked.

Cherry shook her head. "I left the most important thing till last."

Cherry lifted out a parcel wrapped in a bit of carpet. The carpet looked very old, but also very precious. The colours glowed like jewels and glinted with gold threads.

They all watched as Cherry took out what was inside.

"It's just an old *book*!" Billy said.

The book was faded with age and sunlight to a kind of muddy colour. The leather cover was all scuffed and scratched. There were no words or pictures on the front. Mia thought it looked like something in a junk shop.

"I thought it was a magic wand or a sword," Billy moaned.

"No offence, Cherry, but that belongs in the bin," Juno said.

Cherry laughed. "This book has been in my family for hundreds of years. Do you think it would still be here if it looked magic on the *outside*?"

"So it is magic?" Billy whispered.

Cherry's dark eyes sparkled. "It's totally magic! It was my great-great-great-aunty's. Too many greats – so I just call her my aunty."

"Can we see inside?" Billy begged.

"Just a peep," Cherry said.

And she opened the book a tiny bit.

Mia felt a warm breeze ruffle her hair. She smelled sunshine and roses and sweet spices. She heard distant voices and laughter.

Then they heard a closer sound. Someone was coming up the stairs.

Cherry snapped the book shut and the sounds and spicy smells faded away.

"So where's this new foster kid?" a voice demanded.

Mia gasped.

Kyle was standing in the doorway.

Chapter 3

Bad Boy Vibes

Kyle strolled into their room. His pale green eyes lit up and Mia could see he was on the hunt for trouble. Kyle always had to stir things up. He couldn't just join in. He had to pick a fight, smash something, *nick* something.

"So, who's your new friend?" he asked, with a grin at Juno.

"Kyle, this is Cherry – Cherry, this is Kyle."

Juno said it so fast that Mia knew she was desperate for Kyle to go away. So was Mia. She had a million questions about Cherry's magic book, but not with Kyle there.

Only Cherry seemed glad to see him. "Hi, Kyle!" she said, with a smile.

Mia was alarmed that she didn't try to hide the book. Cherry didn't know that Kyle's restless green eyes saw *everything*.

Kyle stuck his hands in his pockets. "Bit of a come-down for you, Cherry, to live with all us low-lifes," he said.

Cherry started to comb the tangles out of her dark hair. "I like it here. It's interesting."

"I'm the only *interesting* person in this dump," Kyle boasted.

"I don't agree," Cherry said.

Kyle's smile vanished. "You don't agree that I'm interesting? *That's* not very nice, Cherry!"

Cherry didn't blink. "You are interesting. But Billy and the others are *special*."

Kyle's face twisted. "Oh, Billy's *special* all right! He's the thickest kid ever. Juno only cares how she looks. And Mia thinks she's too good for the rest of us! Wait till you've been here as long as I have, Cherry. Then see if you still think they're so *special*." And he stormed out.

"People always say I'm thick," Billy said. He put his arms round Mrs Turvey's dog and hid his face so no one could see him cry.

"Kyle will have it in for you now," Juno told Cherry. "Be careful."

Cherry just smiled at Juno. "We're not going to worry about Kyle. I like your nails, Juno. Will you paint mine silver too?"

Juno looked pleased. "Sure!"

Billy sniffed back his tears. "I'll get the nail polish," he said.

Mia stared out the window. She couldn't stop thinking about Kyle's nasty words. She'd only included Kyle in their wish because Juno had told Mia off for hogging all the magic.

So Mia had wished for happy endings for *everybody*, even Kyle. Now she felt like she'd made a big mistake.

"Tea in five minutes!" Mrs Turvey called.

"Wave your hands around! Your nails are still wet!" Juno told Cherry.

"Like this?" Cherry flapped her hands like crazy.

Mia giggled. Kyle had tried to spoil things with his bad boy vibes but Cherry hadn't let him. Mia really liked Cherry. It wasn't just the magic. Cherry was fun, the kind of girl who'd be a fab best friend.

Downstairs, the kitchen was full of good cooking smells. The twins Riley and Rosie were at the table. They stared at Cherry with big round eyes.

Mrs Turvey put a huge home-made pie on the table. "Don't give yours to the dog," she warned Billy.

Kyle came in late. He didn't talk to anybody, just started stuffing food in his mouth.

When the meal was over, Cherry helped Mrs Turvey get the little ones ready for bed. Juno and Mia had to stack the dishwasher.

"What's inside Cherry's book?" Juno whispered. "I think it's spells."

Mia shook her head. "I don't know."

They went up to their room. Cherry's book was on her pillow. Mia and Juno kept looking at it.

Cherry came in so silently that they didn't know she was there until she spoke.

"It's time," she said. She turned to pick up her book.

Then Billy rushed in, wild-eyed. "Kyle says he'll do it tonight!"

"*Billy!*" Mia and Juno moaned.

"Shush!" Cherry said. "What does Kyle say he'll do?"

"He's going to wait till I'm asleep, then he'll nick my diamond!" And Billy sobbed as if his heart would break.

Chapter 4

As many stories as there are stars in the sky

Mia jumped with fright as the bedroom door smashed into the wall.

Kyle barged in. "I knew Billy would blab like a baby. I was just messing, OK? Why would I want a stupid bit of glass?"

Cherry jumped up and put herself between Kyle and Billy. For the first time Mia noticed her T-shirt.

On the front it said in glittery writing –
Cherry Green, Story Queen.

"What's a *story queen* when it's at home?" Kyle jeered.

"Stick around and you might find out!" Cherry told him.

'Please don't,' Mia thought.

"No way!" Kyle said, disgusted. "Stories are for little kids!"

"My aunty wouldn't agree with you," said Cherry, with her friendly smile.

"Your aunty?" Kyle looked blank.

"She was a famous story-teller," Cherry said. "Stories saved my aunty's life."

Juno's eyes were huge. "How?"

Cherry puffed out her cheeks. "It's a bit complicated. Basically, my aunty's parents married her to this king who had a bad habit of killing his brides on their wedding night."

Juno and Mia gasped.

"To be fair, his first bride did run away, and that made him go crazy," Cherry said.

"I can't believe they still made your aunty *marry* him," Mia said.

Cherry nodded. "Me neither. But she was a clever cookie, and she didn't fancy being another dead bride. So every night she told the king the longest, most thrilling story she could think of! Then, when the sun rose, my aunty always stopped the story at the very best part. She hoped the king would be so desperate to hear how it ended that he'd let her live for one more day."

"Did it work?" Juno asked.

"Oh yes! The king stopped being crazy, fell in love with my aunty and they lived happily ever after!"

But Cherry's words made Kyle even more angry. His face twisted up. "Nobody *ever* lives happily ever after! NOBODY! Get it?" He rushed out with a slam of the door.

Mia didn't really notice. She'd been staring at the sparkly words on Cherry's T-shirt. "It's not spells in Cherry's book," she said to Juno. "It's stories! That's why she's the story queen!"

Juno stared at her. "But what good are stories? They're no use at all!"

"Stories *are* useful!" Billy said. "What about Cherry's aunty and that scary king?"

But Mia totally understood what Juno meant. Stories were all very well, but they couldn't make someone live happily ever after. Only a magic spell could do that.

"Are the stories your aunty told the king in that book?" Billy asked.

Cherry nodded. "My aunty's stories plus millions more. My granny gave me this book and she said there were as many stories in it as there are stars in the sky."

"That book isn't big enough for millions of stories," Juno grumped.

Billy grinned. "You *do* know Cherry's aunty's book is magic, don't you?"

Cherry was waiting now with her book on her knee. Her eyes had a faraway look, and that fairy-tale shimmer seemed brighter. When she looked at Cherry now, Mia totally believed her great-great-great-aunty had been a story-teller princess.

Cherry opened the book and for a puzzling moment Mia saw blank pages. Then a printed title appeared – *The Boy Who Talked to Birds*. And then the blank pages filled with words.

Mia felt prickles of excitement as Cherry read, "Once upon a time."

The bedroom filled with the sounds of the forest. Twigs cracked, birds cooed and water trickled over stones. Mia blinked as she looked *through* the pages into another world!

Then Mia gasped as she slipped *inside* the magic book. She was still in the bedroom, next to Juno on Cherry's bed. But she could smell

damp moss and feel the sun on her face. Part of her was *inside* the story!

Billy and Juno gasped too. They were inside the story as well. For a second, Mia panicked. What if they couldn't get back to the real world? Then she thought, 'We can't get lost. We're with Cherry Green, the Story Queen!'

Cherry's voice led them deeper and deeper into the forest. Soon they saw a boy walking all alone. He was homeless and hungry and in disgrace. His parents had sent him to a teacher to learn to be rich and clever. But then the boy came home and they asked him what he'd learned. "I know what the birds say when they sing," he told them. His parents were disgusted. "You stupid boy! Who *cares* what birds sing about?" they said. And they told him to leave home and never come back.

The boy walked for days until he came to a beautiful big city. In the city, the birds were acting very oddly. Blackbirds, sparrows, woodpeckers all flew in and out of houses, beating their wings on windows, crying out in their wild bird voices, trying to make the humans understand them.

The boy instantly knew that the birds were crying out a warning. *"Soldiers are coming! Run and tell the king!"*

He called back to the birds. "I'll tell the king but I'm just a boy. He might not believe me!"

"Then we'll come with you," the birds cried.

Later that day, the king was amazed to see a boy walk in the palace gates with a great cloud of birds above his head. "He must be a powerful wizard," the king said and he rushed out to meet him.

The boy had come just in time. The king listened to the birds' warning, the soldiers were driven away and the kingdom was saved. The boy who talked to birds grew up to become a great hero.

"*And they all lived happily ever after,*" Cherry's voice said.

In an instant Mia was back with the others, feeling as if she had been on a wonderful adventure.

Billy gave a happy sigh. "That boy wasn't stupid. He was a hero."

"His parents were so, *so* wrong!" Juno agreed. Mia could see she was still half inside the story. She'd forgotten she thought stories were useless.

"I liked how that boy had a diamond stud like me," Billy said.

"Did he?" Mia said.

"He *totally* did," Billy said, yawning.

*

In the night Mia shot awake. She thought she'd heard the bedroom door open and close, but perhaps it was only part of her dream.

'I can't wait for Cherry to read us more stories tomorrow,' she thought.

But when morning came, Cherry's book had vanished.

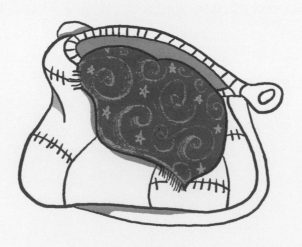

Chapter 5

Lost and Found

Before they went to sleep, Cherry had put her book away safe in its bit of carpet inside her bag. The book thief had left the carpet behind.

Mia picked it up and stroked its glowing colours. The thief had to be Kyle. Who else would have taken Cherry's magic book?

Juno's eyes were full of angry tears. "I knew Kyle would try to get you back."

"It's OK, Juno," Cherry told her.

"Kyle stole your magic book and it's *OK*?" Juno said, astonished.

"I'm pretty sure Kyle will bring it back," Cherry said.

"And that makes it OK, does it?" Juno choked. "Sneaking in while we're asleep. Nicking your book! I'm *ashamed* of him!"

Mia was ashamed of Kyle too. 'Why did we include him in our wish?' she thought. 'Kyle doesn't deserve to have a happy ending.' She wanted to cry.

Juno gave Cherry a strange look. "You *knew* Kyle would take it, didn't you?"

"I had a feeling that's what he'd do," Cherry said.

"Then why didn't you hide it?" Juno demanded.

"Because I knew he'd bring it back," Cherry said.

"But it's your magic book!" Juno said. "Kyle could put it in a bin, or set it on fire. He's not nice, Cherry!"

"He'll bring it back," Cherry repeated.

Mia stared at her, astonished. It was like Cherry *trusted* Kyle, like she knew something about him they didn't.

At first it seemed that Cherry was wrong. Kyle wasn't at breakfast or lunch or tea.

Mia heard Mrs Turvey on the phone. "He's never missed a meal before," she was saying. "He's a good boy really."

Mia hoped he wouldn't come back. Life was better without Kyle making trouble for everyone.

Mia and Juno were in their bedroom playing dominoes with Billy, when the door was flung open and Kyle strode in.

"What are you playing at, tricking little kids?" Kyle demanded. He shoved Cherry's book under her nose. He had brought it back, but he looked as if he wanted to hit someone.

"Who did I trick?" Cherry asked.

'Everybody! Always going on about story queens and happy endings. It's *blank*!" Kyle flicked through the pages. "Blank, blank, blank. No story. No happy endings. Just BLANK!"

"It seems that way, I know –" Cherry started.

"Because it *is* that way," Kyle yelled.

Cherry stood up so they were face to face. She didn't get angry or upset. She didn't raise her voice. "Listen, Kyle, you can steal my aunty's book, but you can't steal the stories inside. Magic doesn't work like that."

"Stop going on about magic, will you? It's all *tricks*!" Kyle almost threw the book at Cherry. Mia was shocked to see tears in his eyes.

In her mind, Mia saw Kyle sneaking Cherry's book out of the house. She saw him opening it and then closing it and opening it again, hoping to find magic, hoping for a happy ending, but finding nothing but blank pages.

"Everyone at Mrs Turvey's wants to live happily ever after," Billy had said. But Mia had made up her mind that Kyle was different. Until this moment, she had never thought that this angry boy could share her own hopes and dreams.

Kyle was half way out of the room when Cherry called his name. "Thank you for bringing my aunty's book back," she said.

Kyle stopped. Mia thought he was going to say something, but then he just slouched off to his room.

Minutes later two curly little heads appeared – Riley and Rosie. "It's nearly our bedtime, so we've come for our story," Rosie said to Cherry.

Cherry read them a story about a bunch of daft animals who ran around telling everyone that the sky was falling in. Riley and Rosie were only four years old so for them it was perfectly normal to go inside a story and meet talking ducks and hens. They were spellbound.

When the twins had gone to bed, Juno said, "Hurray! Now for some proper story time!"

She went to shut the door, but Cherry stopped her. "Leave it open a bit," she said.

'So Kyle can listen,' Mia thought.

By the time Cherry finished the story, the moon was rising and Billy was fast asleep.

Mia gazed out at the night sky, but part of her was still inside a world of magical beasts, evil step-mothers and flying carpets.

Cherry took out the bit of carpet and began to put her book away.

All of a sudden Billy woke up. "Once upon a time, was that part of a real flying carpet?" he asked.

Cherry put her fingers to her lips and gave him a tiny nod, as if it was their secret.

Billy's eyes went huge. "It IS!"

"Come on, Billy, bedtime," Juno said.

Just then Mia heard a sudden scuffle on the landing. But when Juno opened the door nobody was there.

Chapter 6

The Robber Prince

It was Cherry's last night at Mrs Turvey's.

They had spent the day doing fun summer things. They'd gone to the adventure playground, picked strawberries at the city farm, then helped Mrs Turvey make strawberry shortcake for pudding.

Kyle had gone off for the afternoon with his mates. He was home for tea, but he kept his head down and only said "yes" or "no" if anyone spoke to him.

When evening came, Cherry said, "How about we make big comfy heaps of pillows and cushions on the floor?"

When they'd finished, she said, "Now my aunty would feel at home. It's like Persia in the old days!"

They settled down. Billy leaned against Cherry and she began a story called *The Robber Prince*.

In a heartbeat, Mia was inside the world of the story. An evil wizard wanted revenge on the king and queen, so he stole their new baby son. Then he left the crying baby on a heap of leaves in the forest, all alone. Night came. Mia gasped as she saw huge yellow eyes glowing in the dark. It was a pack of hungry wolves!

Mia heard the wolves panting. She smelled their hot meaty breath as they padded closer and closer to the baby. Then at that exact moment she sensed Kyle in the door.

Part of Mia was in the story, sick with terror, watching the wolves sniff the baby prince all over. Another part of her was watching Kyle. For the first time ever, his pale green eyes were still. *All* of Kyle was still. He was listening so hard to the story he had almost stopped breathing.

Kyle edged closer and closer. Now he was inside the story with Mia and the others, watching amazed as a she-wolf washed the lost baby with her long tongue.

Time passed and winter came to the fairy-tale forest. The baby was a toddler now, rolling in the snow with the wolf cubs. Then a gun shot rang out. The wolves fled. A band of robbers appeared among the trees!

Cherry told them how the robbers took the little prince to their hide-out in the mountains, where he grew up to be the biggest, boldest robber of them all. He had many adventures where he fooled his enemies with his robber's cunning. But, deep inside, the robber was still a prince with a good and noble heart. In his last adventure he defeated the wizard who had stolen him from the palace as a baby. Then he set free all the people the wizard had taken prisoner over the years.

When at last the story ended, Mia couldn't move. Juno and Billy were in a kind of dream. They had been alone in the forest, licked by a she-wolf, adopted by a band of robbers, and defeated a wicked wizard. Now they were back in Mrs Turvey's front bedroom and it was almost dark.

Then Mia looked at Kyle and was amazed to see the same dreamy look on his face. He took a deep breath as if he was coming back from somewhere far, far away.

Cherry was watching Kyle too. He looked up and met her eyes.

For a long moment nobody spoke.

Then Kyle said, "How about reading us one of those stories your aunty told that crazy king?"

Mia saw Juno give a happy little shiver as Cherry opened the book at a new story.

'Everyone's different now,' Mia thought.

Cherry hadn't waved a wand over Mrs Turvey's house to make everyone live happily ever after. She had done something even more magic. She had turned four random foster kids into heroes.

Together they had climbed glass mountains, outsmarted monsters and magic imps and they had come back stronger, braver, *changed*. Even Kyle. Kyle wasn't angry Kyle any more – the stories had changed him, the same way they'd changed the crazy king who married Cherry's aunty. Mia could see it in Kyle's eyes. He was a king's son who'd got lost, a robber prince, a bad boy hero with a good heart.

It was Mia's turn to give a happy shiver as Cherry turned to a new page and said, "Once upon a time …"

Chapter 7

Gold Threads

Mia never heard how the last story ended. She fell fast asleep while Cherry was still reading.

She woke in the pale light of a new day to hear someone open Mrs Turvey's gate. Mia flew to the window and saw Cherry walking down the street, her patchwork bag over her arm.

She wanted to bang on the window so Cherry would turn round and see her. She wanted to shout, "Come back!" Cherry had told them she would leave after three days, but Mia had hoped she would stay. Not for ever, but as long as they needed her.

Kyle came up behind her. "What's up?" Then he saw Cherry too and said, "Oh, she's gone already."

"She never said goodbye," Mia said in a shaky voice.

They watched in silence until Cherry disappeared round a corner.

"I'm scared I'll forget." Kyle's voice was shaky too. "Like I'll think we made it all up." Kyle looked crumpled and tired and unhappy.

"I'm scared I'll forget too," Mia told him.

In stories, heroes came back from their adventures with pockets full of rubies, or a princess for their bride. But real life wasn't like that. In real life people didn't even always say goodbye.

"Where's Cherry?" Billy appeared beside them in his PJs.

"What do you mean, where's Cherry?" Juno scrambled up, rubbing her eyes.

Mia gave a sad nod. "Someone must have made a wish."

I'm only staying for three days. Like a magic whirlwind, Cherry Green, Story Queen, had come and gone.

"Has she left us something to remember her by?" Billy was trying to be brave, but his voice sounded very small.

"Cherry? All she had was her clothes and her book!" Juno said.

Billy dropped on his hands and knees. "She *did* leave us something!" His hands were full of gold threads and his eyes shone. "You know what these are? Magic threads from a real flying carpet. Cherry told me!"

Kyle took a deep breath. Was he getting ready to make fun of Billy? Then he said, in a kind voice, "Threads from a flying carpet, yeah? That's got to be worth having!"

"Give them to me, Billy," Juno said. "I've got an idea. I'll need your help, Mia!"

After breakfast Juno and Mia begged Mrs Turvey for some bright silk threads. Over the next few days the girls worked on their secret project. While they worked they talked about Cherry, and how they both used to feel like they were in the wrong story with no hope of a happy ending.

"But I don't feel like I'm in the wrong story any more," Mia said.

"Nor me," Juno agreed.

At last their secret project was finished.

One morning, Juno and Mia woke up all the others and took them out into the misty garden. Juno handed over five friendship bracelets, one for every foster kid at Mrs Turvey's. She kept the sixth bracelet for herself.

Kyle stared at his bracelet. His face was totally blank.

'He hates it,' Mia thought.

Then Kyle looked up with an amazed smile. "I'll never forget her now, will I?"

Mia almost fainted with relief. "That's what me and Juno thought!"

Mia was really proud of her and Juno's work. Each bracelet had a sparkly gold thread from a flying carpet. A thread of magic.

Our books are tested
for children and young people by
children and young people.

Thanks to everyone who consulted on
a manuscript for their time and effort in
helping us to make our books better
for our readers.